CONTENTS

The Daring Dragon   4

The Kingdom Under the Sea   23

Notes on Magical Tales from   46
China and Japan

THE DARING DRAGON

There are hundreds of dragons in China. Every pool and river has its own, and there are a quite a few more in the sea. They are not fierce, and they don't eat people either – which is just as well, seeing as there are such a lot of them. But *why* are there so many dragons in China?

4

Long ago, in China, there was a flood. It was the same kind of flood as the one in the Bible, when Noah built his big boat. But in China some of the people and animals were saved by two great heroes, some magic clay, and, of course, Chinese dragons come into the story too.

The Yellow Emperor, supreme god of the heavens, was angry. "People keep on doing bad, wicked things," he said. "I'm going to get rid of them! And I'm going to do it now!" So he ordered the rain god to make endless rain.

The rain god was mightily pleased and rushed off across the sky, whipping up big black clouds and throwing down torrents of rain. He didn't stop for a moment. He loved his work.

And so, on earth, it rained endlessly, and there was a great flood. Houses,

plants and trees were swept away, and thousands of people and animals were drowned. A few families ran up into the mountains and managed to survive. But even they were afraid as every day they saw the flood water rise higher.

Only one god – Kun, grandson of the Yellow Emperor – looked down from the heavens and was truly sorry for the people. He went to his grandfather's palace and pleaded with him. "Lord of the Heavens," he said. "Stop the endless rain. Do not let any more people die."

But the Yellow Emperor was still angry, and he simply closed his eyes, drew in a deep breath and turned away.

As Kun walked out of the palace, sadly shaking his head, an old black tortoise came plodding towards him.

"What's the matter?" asked the tortoise.

"I don't want any more people to drown," said Kun. "But I don't know how to help them."

"Magic mud! That's what you need!" said the tortoise. "Just sprinkle some on the flood water and watch what happens next!"

"Where can I get this mud?" asked Kun.

"Easy!" said the tortoise. "The Yellow Emperor has a big jarful in his treasure house."

"But he won't give me any," said Kun. "He doesn't want the flood to end."

"Then…" said the tortoise, and he dropped his voice to a whisper, "then… you'll have to steal some!"

Kun was a god. In a moment he was inside his grandfather's treasure house.

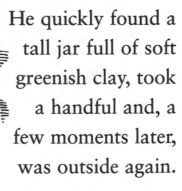

He quickly found a tall jar full of soft greenish clay, took a handful and, a few moments later, was outside again.

He thought, and next thing he was on earth, standing on a mountainside, with that endless rain spattering down on his head. He broke off a small piece of the mud, and sprinkled it on the flood water. It truly was *magic mud*! It doubled in size, doubled again, and yet again. It kept on growing, *and*, at the same time, it soaked up water, like a sponge. Before long there was an island.

Kun worked fast, travelling from place to place, sprinkling magic mud on the water, making more islands and big land bridges between the mountains. People crept out from the caves and huts where they sheltered and watched him. At last they had a little hope...maybe the flood would not cover everything.

12

But the rain still fell, and besides, before Kun had used up all the mud, the Yellow Emperor looked and he saw everything. "Kun must die!" said the Yellow Emperor, and he ordered the god of fire to do the deed.

When Kun saw the fire god coming, he changed himself into a white horse and tried to hide among some boulders at the top of a mountain. But the fire god hurled a lightning flash, and Kun, the white horse, fell down as if he were dead.

13

Time passed. Kun, the white horse, stirred. Something was growing inside him. He shuddered, and from out of his body sprang a new life – a golden dragon – young, strong and splendid.

Then Kun, the brave hero, finally died. But his son, who called himself Yu, flew up to the heavens. He entered the palace of the Yellow Emperor, bowed his dragon head and spoke softly and respectfully.

"Great Lord of the Heavens," he said. "I am Yu, the son of Kun, sent into the world to finish his work. Honoured Great-Grandfather, the people have suffered much and are sad. Take pity on them and stop the endless rain."

The Yellow Emperor listened. His anger cooled. "Golden Dragon," he said, "from now on you shall be the rain god. But that is not enough. I must give you some magic mud to make new land and soak up the extra water."

The Yellow Emperor pointed to a
tortoise standing in the corner, listening.
It was the same old black tortoise who
had helped Kun! "You may take," said
the Yellow Emperor, and he smiled,
"as much magic mud as can be piled on
top of that tortoise's back."

Yu, the golden dragon, bowed his head.
"I thank you, Great-Grandfather," he said.

There was much to do. Swiftly Yu flew off. He broke up the clouds and chased and blew them away. While he was doing this, he came face to face with the old rain god, who was exceedingly cross. He had enjoyed making endless rain, and he didn't want to give up his job. But the Yellow Emperor had to be obeyed. All the rain god could do was grumble and complain.

When the rain at last stopped falling, Yu piled some magic mud on the tortoise's back, and then the two of them came down to earth.

17

Still there was much to do. Yu and the tortoise travelled through the land of China, sprinkling magic mud, making new land, and at the same time soaking up the flood waters.

When all the magic mud had been used, Yu said to the tortoise, "Only one thing left to do! We must make some rivers!"

Then, with the tortoise leading the way, the golden dragon used his tail to plough

deep furrows across the soft, muddy soil, from the mountains to the sea.

It was quite easy. There was only one difficult bit. When Yu was ploughing the course of the Yellow River, in Northern China, he came to a place where some big, rocky cliffs stood in the way. Yu thought for a moment, then he turned round and lashed the rocks with his tail and cut a great chasm through them.

"This place shall be called Dragon's Gate," he said. "It will always be sacred to dragons."

In this way Yu, the golden dragon, made the great rivers which flow across China today. It is said also that when the cold, sad, hungry people ventured out of the caves and huts in the mountains, where they had sheltered during the endless rain, they asked Yu to be their emperor. And so Yu, the golden dragon, became a man-god, and lived on earth. Yu is still honoured and remembered, especially at Dragon's Gate on the Yellow River.

There, each spring, when the fish swim
upstream, they must leap over the fast-
flowing rapids that cascade down the
chasm which Yu cut with his tail. The fish
that leap through the wild foaming spray
and clear the rapids in one enormous
leap – those fish change into dragons and
continue their leap up to the clouds. There
they frolic and play in the summertime,
before returning to the rivers and pools
where they sleep in the winter.

Dragons live a long, long time, and every year at Dragon's Gate a few more dragons are born. And that is why there are so many dragons in China.

A Chinese tale

THE KINGDOM UNDER THE SEA

One summer evening, long ago, a lad called Urashima Taro was walking across the beach after a day's fishing when he saw a turtle lying helpless on its back, slowly waving its flippers. So he bent down and picked it up.

"You poor creature," he said, "I wonder who turned you upside down and left you here to die in the sun? Some thoughtless young children who knew no better, I suppose."

He carried the turtle over the sands and waded out into the sea, as deep as he could, before lowering it into the water. And as he let it go, he called out, "Off you go, venerable turtle – and may you live for a thousand years!"

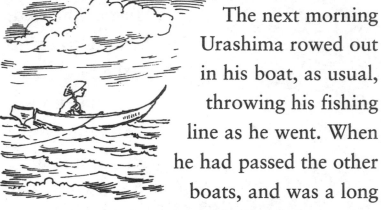

The next morning Urashima rowed out in his boat, as usual, throwing his fishing line as he went. When he had passed the other boats, and was a long way out at sea and all alone, he took a rest and let the boat drift on the waves.

It was then that he heard someone softly calling: "Urashima! Urashima Taro!"

He looked round, but there was not another boat in sight. Then he heard again: "Urashima! Urashima Taro!" It seemed to come from close by. So he looked again, and he saw a turtle, swimming beside the boat.

"Turtle," he said, "was it you who called my name just now?" "Yes, honourable fisherman, I was the one who spoke," answered the turtle. "Yesterday you saved my life, and today I have come to thank you and offer to take you to Ryn Jin, the palace of the Dragon King Under the Sea, who is my father."

Urashima was astonished. "The Dragon King Under the Sea is your father?" he said. "Surely not!"

"It is true. I am his daughter," she answered. "And if you climb on my back, I will take you to him."

Urashima thought that it would be a fine thing to see the kingdom under the sea, so he climbed out of the boat and sat himself down on the turtle's back.

Immediately they were off, skimming across the waves. And when it seemed they could go no faster, the turtle dived down into the depths of the sea. For a long time they sped through the water, passing whales and sharks, playful dolphins and shoals of silvery fish.

At last Urashima saw in the distance
a magnificent coral gate decorated
with pearls and glittering gems, and
beyond it the long sloping roofs and
gables of a coral palace.

"We are approaching the gateway of
my father's palace," said the turtle, and

even as she spoke, they reached it. "Now, from here, please, you must walk."

She turned to a swordfish who was the keeper of the gate and said, "This is an honoured guest from the land of Japan. Please show him the way to go." And with that she swam off.

The swordfish led Urashima into
an outer courtyard where a great
company of fish, row upon row of
octopus and cuttlefish, bonito and plaice,
bowed graciously towards him.

"Welcome to Ryn Jin, the palace of
the Dragon King Under the Sea!" they
chorused. "Welcome and thrice welcome!"

Then the great company of
fish escorted Urashima
through to an inner
courtyard that led to
the great door of
the coral palace.
The door opened
and there stood
a radiantly
beautiful
princess. She
wore flowing
garments of red
and green, shot
through with all
the colours of a
wave with sunlight
on it, and her long
black hair streamed over
her shoulders in the style of long ago.

31

"I welcome you to my father's kingdom," she said, "and ask you to stay here for a while in the land of everlasting youth, where summer never dies and sorrow never comes."

As Urashima listened to her words and gazed at her beautiful face, a feeling of contentment flooded over him. "My only wish is that I might stay here with you in this land for ever," he said. "Then I shall be your bride and we shall live together always," said the princess. "But first we must ask my father for his permission."

The princess took him by the hand and led him through long corridors to her father's great hall. There they knelt before the mighty lord, the Dragon King Under the Sea, and bowed so low that their foreheads touched the floor.

"Honourable father," said the princess, "this is the youth who saved my life in the land of men. If it pleases you, he is the one that I have chosen to be my husband."

"It pleases me," the Dragon King answered, "but what does the fisher-lad say? Does he accept?"

"Oh...I gladly accept," said Urashima.

So then there was a wedding feast. And when the princess and Urashima had pledged their love, three times three, with a wedding cup of saké wine, the entertainments began.

Soft music was played, and strange and wonderful rainbow-coloured fish danced and sang.

The next day, when the celebrations were over, the princess showed Urashima some of the marvels of her father's coral palace and his kingdom. The greatest of these was the garden of the four seasons.

To the east lay the garden of spring, where the plum and cherry were in full blossom and birds of all kinds sang sweetly. To the south the trees were clothed in the green of summer and the crickets chirruped lazily.

In the west the
autumn maples
were ablaze with
flame-coloured
leaves and the
chrysanthemums
bloomed. While in
the north
stood the winter
garden where the
bamboos and
the earth were
covered in snow,
and the ponds
were thick with ice.

Now there were so many things to see
and wonder at in the kingdom under the
sea that Urashima forgot about his own
home and his old life. But after a few
days, he remembered his parents.

He said to the princess, "By now my mother and father must think that I have been drowned at sea. It must be three days or more since I left them. I must go, immediately, and tell them what has happened."

"Wait," she said. "Wait a little longer. Stay at least one more day, here with me."

"It is my duty to go and see my parents," he answered. "But I will return to you."

"Then I must become a turtle again and carry you to the land above the waves," she said. "But, before you leave, accept this gift from me." And the princess gave him a beautiful, three-tiered lacquer box, tied round with a red silk cord.

"Keep this box with you always, but do not open it, whatever happens."

And Urashima promised that he would not open the box.

Once again the princess became a turtle, Urashima sat astride her back, and they were off. For a long time they rode through the sea, and then, at last, they soared upwards and reached the waves. Urashima turned his face towards the land and saw again the mountains and the bay he knew so well.

They came to the beach,
and he stepped ashore.

"Remember," said
the turtle. "Do not
open the box."

"I will remember,"
he said.

He walked across the
sands and took the path that led to his
home. But as he looked around, a strange
fear came over him. The trees somehow
looked different. So did the houses. And
he didn't recognise anyone he saw. When
he reached his own
house, it too looked
different. Only the
little stream in the
garden and a few
stepping stones
were the same.

40

He called: "Mother! Father!" And an old man whom he had never seen before opened the door.

"Who are you?" asked Urashima. "And where are my mother and father? And what has happened to our house? Everything has changed. And yet it is only three days since I, Urashima Taro, lived here."

"This is my house," said the old man "and it was my father's and my father's father's before him. But I have heard that a man called  Urashima Taro once lived here. The story goes that one day he went fishing and didn't come back, and then, not long after, his old parents died of sorrow. But that was about three hundred years ago."

Urashima shook his head. It was hard to believe that his mother and father, and 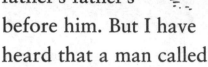 all his friends too, had died long, long ago. He thanked the old man and walked slowly back to the shore and sat down on the sands.

He felt sad. "Three hundred years,"
he thought. "Three hundred years must
be only three days in the kingdom under
the sea."

Now as he sat there, he held the lacquer
box the princess had given him in his
hands, and his fingers idly played with the
red silk cord. And the cord came undone.
Without thinking what he was doing, he
opened the first box. Three soft wisps of
smoke came swirling out and curled
around him, and the handsome youth
became an old, old man.

He opened the second box. There was a mirror inside it, and he looked and saw that his hair was grey and his face was wrinkled. He opened the third box. A crane's feather drifted out, brushed across his face and settled on his head, and the old man changed into a bird – a beautiful, elegant crane.

The crane flew up and looked out over the sea, and he saw a turtle, floating on the waves, close to the shore. The turtle looked up, and she saw the crane. And then she knew that her husband, Urashima Taro, would never ever return to her father's kingdom under the sea.

A Japanese tale

THE DARING DRAGON

A Chinese Tale

Like the European folktale dragon, the Chinese dragon has scales and, although it usually has no wings, it too can fly. While the European dragon is traditionally wicked, eats people, breathes fire and must be conquered by a knightly hero, the Chinese dragon is good. As in this tale, *The Daring Dragon*, it is also linked with water, instead of fire. In winter it sleeps in pools or rivers and when it wakes, it flies up to the skies, where dragons gather to fight, play and make summer rains. Sometimes they stay up there too long, and then there are floods.

This tale can be compared with the Bible story of Noah and the flood. God and the Chinese Yellow Emperor make a flood to get rid of humans because they are being so wicked. But the ark Noah makes in the Bible and the islands of magic mud in this tale are safe places, so not everything is destroyed. Both stories end with hope and a promise for the future – Noah sees a rainbow arching across the sky, while in the Chinese tale the rain god is replaced by fish that leap up into the clouds as rain dragons.

THE KINGDOM UNDER THE SEA

A Japanese Tale

As in most magical tales, Urashima Taro's kind deed of rescuing a turtle is generously rewarded in *The Kingdom Under the Sea*. Urashima is taken for a ride on the turtle's back, visits a fabulous underwater kingdom and finally marries the turtle, who is really a princess. He is right in wanting to see his parents and tell them he is alive, but he spoils everything by breaking his promise and opening the beautiful box. In most versions of this Japanese tale, the box contains only mist and when the hero opens it, he grows old immediately and dies. This version has a slightly happier ending.

In the story, Urashima Taro thinks he has been away from home for three days, but it has been three hundred years and everything has changed. A similar thing happens in *Rip Van Winkle*, a North American tale. When out walking, Rip meets some odd-looking men. He accepts a drink from them and falls asleep. When he wakes, he finds his village and the people have changed. He has been asleep for twenty years. Everyone is amazed, and Rip becomes a local celebrity!

MAGICAL TALES
from
AROUND THE WORLD

Retold by Margaret Mayo ✳ *Illustrated by Peter Bailey*

PEGASUS AND THE PROUD PRINCE
and The Flying Carpet   ISBN 1 84362 086 3   £3.99

UNANANA AND THE ENORMOUS ELEPHANT
and The Feathered Snake   ISBN 1 84362 087 1   £3.99

THE FIERY PHOENIX
and The Lemon Princess   ISBN 1 84362 088 X   £3.99

THE GIANT SEA SERPENT
and The Unicorn   ISBN 1 84362 089 8   £3.99

THE MAN-EATING MINOTAUR
and The Magic Fruit   ISBN 1 84362 090 1   £3.99

THE MAGICAL MERMAID
and Kate Crackernuts   ISBN 1 84362 091 X   £3.99

THE INCREDIBLE THUNDERBIRD
and Baba Yaga Bony-legs   ISBN 1 84362 092 8   £3.99

THE DARING DRAGON
and The Kingdom Under the Sea   ISBN 1 84362 093 6   £3.99

Orchard Myths are available from all good bookshops,
or can be ordered direct from the publisher:
Orchard Books, PO BOX 29, Douglas IM99 1BQ
Credit card orders please telephone 01624 836000
or fax 01624 837033
or e-mail: bookshop@enterprise.net for details.

To order please quote title, author and ISBN
and your full name and address.
Cheques and postal orders should be
made payable to 'Bookpost plc'.
Postage and packing is FREE within the UK
(overseas customers should add £1.00 per book).

Prices and availability are subject to change.